A True Blue Idea

A complete listing of the books in this series can be found online at wsupress.wayne.edu

A True Blue Idea

Marina Colasanti
Translated by Adria Frizzi

Wayne State University Press
Detroit

ISBN 978-0-8143-4639-6 (hardcover)

Library of Congress Control Number: 2018963276

Published with the assistance of a fund established by Thelma Gray James of Wayne State University for the publication of folklore and English studies.

Wayne State University Press
Leonard N. Simons Building
4809 Woodward Avenue
Detroit, Michigan 48201–1309

Visit us online at wsupress.wayne.edu

For
Fabiana and Alessandra,
my fairies

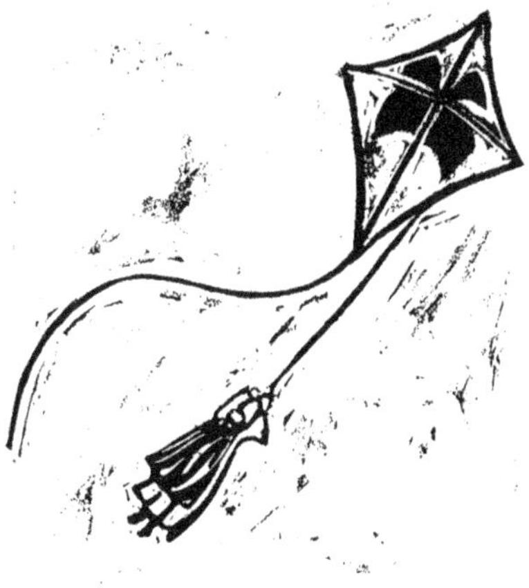

Contents

The Book by Marina Colasanti 1

The Last King 3

Through the Hoop 7

For a Pair of Velvet Wings 11

A Thorn of Ivory 15

A True Blue Idea 21

Among the Leaves So Green O 27

Thread by Thread 33

The One and Only 37

Seven Years and Seven More 43

News and Honey 49

Afterword by Adria Frizzi 53

Works by Marina Colasanti in English 63

The Book

This is a book of fairy tales, with swans, unicorns, and princesses. And before anyone is put off by the subject matter in a world of advanced space technology, I think it's important to make clear that my interests and explorations gravitate toward that timeless thing called the unconscious.

There is no single age or story for emotions. Nor did I wish to address people of one particular size or another as I attempted to put these emotions on paper. I only concerned myself with erecting these symbolic constructions, certain that the material I was dealing with was timeless and would resonate with others.

Perhaps it would have been more convenient and easier to create narratives apt to seduce with their modernity or impress with their everyday realism. Fairies, I know, are dismissed by many as both alienated and alienating because they are too removed from the twentieth century. But I also know that pumpkins never turned into carriages, not even when carriages were the fastest means of conveyance. External reality changes. But our internal reality, comprised of fears and fantasies, remains the same. And it is with the latter that fairies establish a dialogue by interacting symbolically, at any age, and at all times.

Marina Colasanti

The Last King

Every day Kubla Khan, the last king of the Mogul dynasty, climbed to the highest walls of his fortress to meet with the wind.

The wind came from far away and had the whole world to talk about.

Kubla Khan had never left his fortress, he knew nothing of the world. He listened to the words of the wind and learned.

"The Earth is smooth and round," said the wind. "I move ever forward, yet always return to the place where I began. I've traveled around the Earth so many times that it's wound up in my breath."

Kubla Khan thought it must be nice to come and go without ever getting lost.

One day the wind came colder, on its way back from the mountains.

"I went to comb the snow," the wind whispered icily in the king's ear. "Snow is soft and heavy. Beneath its silence the seeds prepare themselves for spring. Only white flowers pierce snow. Only white tracks mark snow. In snow dwells the King of Sleep."

Kubla Khan longed for snow. So he fastened silver threads to the moon and raised it against the wind. From up above the moon, mirror of the cold, brought snow to Kubla Khan. And a peaceful sleep.

Every day, atop the walls of the fortress, the wind talked about its travels.

Every day the king's long hair played in the wind and gathered its sounds like a harp.

The wind talked about the desert.

"The desert," it said with fiery tongue, "is languid like the wheat field. And like the wheat field it obeys me. It, too, bows beneath my hand. But its grain isn't as sweet as wheat. And you don't make loaves out of sand. The desert's drops are called dates."

Kubla Khan longed to sweat with the sweetness of dates. So he fastened threads of gold to the rays of the sun and raised it against the wind. From up above, the heat poured over Kubla Khan's

kingdom, ripening fruit everywhere. And the king drank the juice from his cupped hands.

From atop the walls of the fortress, worn from the wind's endless battering, the entire world lay at the king's feet.

Finally the day came when the wind placed a salty kiss on Kubla Khan's lips, bringing the sea to him.

"The sea is greater than the desert and deeper than snow," sang the wind. "The sea is green like the meadows, but its grass grows in its depths and no one sees the cattle that graze on it. The sea calls out to men and sings. Its voice is named siren."

Did Kubla Khan hear the call of the siren in the wind's voice?

No one knows.

The shepherds of the plains say they saw him fastening flaxen strings to the corners of the great silk kite. Then he raised the kite against the wind and, as his feet lifted from the highest wall of his fortress, he let the white string carry him, the last Mogul king, far up into the sky, where it turns the color of the sea.

Through the Hoop

She began with a green thread. She did not know what to embroider, but she was sure about the green—bright green.

Grass. That's what appeared after the first few stitches. Tall grass, its tips bent as if it were looking at something.

It's looking at the flowers, she thought. And chose a red skein.

Thus, little by little, without an outline, a garden began to appear on the embroidery hoop. It obeyed her hands, it obeyed her fancy, and it grew as if the night dew made it sprout.

Every morning the girl ran to the hoop, looked at it, smiled, and added another bird, a bee, a cricket hidden behind a stem.

The sun shone on the girl's embroidery.

And the garden was so beautiful that she began to like it more than anything else.

It was on the day of the tree. The tree was finished, nothing seemed to be missing. But the girl knew it was time to add the fruit. She embroidered a shiny, purple fruit, like nothing she had ever seen before. And then another, and another, until the tree was drooping, until the tree was bountiful, and her mouth filled with desire for that fruit, never tasted before.

The girl did not know how it happened. The next instant, she was sitting astride the highest branch of the tree, picking fruit and wiping the juice from her mouth.

It must have happened through the thread, she thought when it was time to return home. She looked around, the last fruit was not ready yet, she touched the final stitch in the thread. And there she was, back home.

Now that she knew the way, the girl went down into the embroidery every day. First she chose what she would like to see—a butterfly, a praying mantis. She embroidered with care, then she followed the thread down onto the back of the insect and flew with it until she came to rest on the flowers, and laughed and played and lay in the grass.

The embroidery was nearly done. Hardly any cloth showed through the brightly colored thread. Soon it would be finished.

It needs a heron, she thought. And she chose a white skein with pink hues. She embroidered her stitches with care, knowing, as she inserted the needle, how soft the feathers would be, how gentle the beak. Then she went down to meet her new friend.

It was like that, standing next to the heron, caressing its neck, that her older sister saw her when she leaned over the hoop. She was the only thing that hadn't been embroidered. And the design was so pretty that her sister picked up the needle, the basket of thread, and began to embroider.

She embroidered the girl's hair, and the wind stopped blowing in it. She embroidered her skirt, and the pleats ceased to move. She embroidered her hands, and they froze forever on the heron's neck. She wanted to embroider her feet, but they were hidden in the grass. She wanted to embroider her face, but it was hidden in the shadows. Then she embroidered the ribbon in the girl's hair, finished the stitch, and very carefully cut the thread.

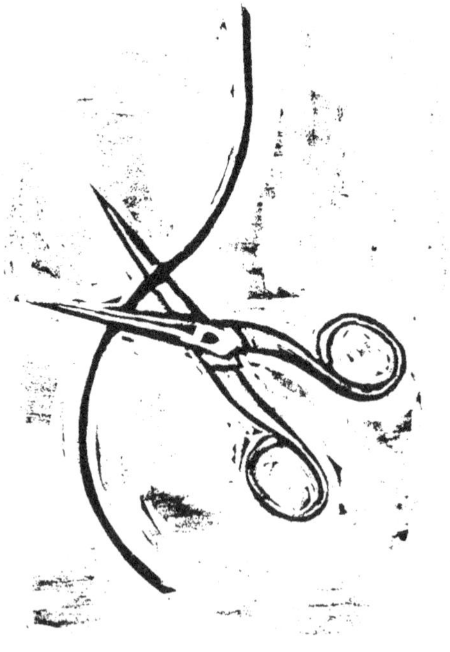

For a Pair of Velvet Wings

The princess took the net, the glass jar, and the box of pins and went hunting. Ever in search of butterflies, she wasn't content with the ones she already had, glass case upon glass case in every room of the palace. She wanted others. She wanted more. She wanted them all.

There was no point in looking in the gardens. After so much hunting, so many pins stuck in their backs, the butterflies knew that was no place for them, and even the caterpillars dragged their lazy undulations away in search of a safer spot to turn into butterflies. Perhaps in the fields, when the harvest was ready. But it was fall. Perhaps in the woods.

And to the woods the princess did go. She searched all morning. She saw two colored wings fluttering among the leaves, threw the net, but only caught a flower stirring in the wind. She thought she had found a dark butterfly resting on a tree trunk—it was a leaf carried by an ant. Then nothing else. Birds, bees, salamanders went about their business undisturbed, flitting around in the sun. But butterflies—none. As if, warned by her presence, they were waiting, hidden at the edge of darkness.

It was almost night when she saw it, a huge black moth fluttering across the dimming blue. She ran after it, trying to keep up. She stumbled on a rock, lost herself in the underbrush. The sky was clear—where was the moth? She thought she'd seen it going one way. She went there. But everything was quiet, just the water rippling on the surface of the lake.

That night, back at the palace, she talked of nothing else. She wanted the moth. If she could have it, she vowed, she'd give up hunting forever. She chose the best spot in her room for it: above the bed, its wings spread over the headboard.

She dreamed about the moth. She was flying with it, reclining on its back, and its velvet wings caressed her as they beat.

At daybreak she armed herself with bow and arrows and went to the woods. She lay on the ground, motionless, waiting, in the same place as the day before. The morning passed. The afternoon

passed. The night blew in its wind. And with the night wind came the black moth.

This time she wasn't going to lose it. Without taking her eyes off it, without making a false move, the princess crept forward through the trees to the edge of the lake. And she saw it descend, spread its large wings, and with a final effort alight without breaking the surface of the water, not moth but swan, a noble black swan.

The water quavers. The princess sets an arrow in her bow, draws back the string, shoots the golden shaft into the swan's breast.

But it is from her own breast that the blood spills. And trickles, and gushes, soaking her clothes, dissolving the silk everywhere it flows, transforming her body into feathers, black velvet feathers.

The day sinks into sleep. On the lake two black swans glide side by side. The golden bow gleams, forgotten.

A Thorn of Ivory

The sun rose and there was the unicorn, grazing in the princess's garden. From among the flowers it gazed up at the window of the room where she came to greet the day. It waited until it saw her at the balcony, and when her delicate foot touched the first step of the stairs leading down to the garden, the unicorn fled into the darkness of the forest.

One day, while visiting his daughter in her chambers early in the morning, the king saw the unicorn in the lily patch.

I must have that animal. And he immediately ordered the hunt.

Day after day the king and his knights hunted the unicorn through the fields and forests. The horses galloped, the hounds ran, and, just when they were all sure they had surrounded it, they lost its scent, got off on the wrong track.

Night after night the king and his knights camped around the fire, listening to the unicorn's crystal-clear whinny in the darkness.

Then, one day, it was gone. Not a track, not a sign of its presence. And silence at night.

Disappointed, the king gave orders to return to the castle.

And as soon as he arrived he went to his daughter's room to tell her what had happened. The princess, saddened by her father's failure, promised that in three moons she would present him with the unicorn.

For the next three nights she wove a golden net out of her hair. Each morning she watched the lily patch in the garden. And on the fourth day, at dawn, when the first light of the sun filled the white blossoms, she threw her net and trapped the unicorn.

Caught in the golden mesh, the unicorn looked upon the one he loved most, now his mistress, who knew nothing of him.

The princess drew closer. What animal was this, with eyes so meek, held by the artifice of her tresses? Velvet hide, lacquered hooves and, sprouting in the center of his brow, the single horn pointing to the sky.

A gentle unicorn tongue licked the hand that held him. The princess shuddered, loosened the net, the unicorn rose up on his slender legs.

How long did it take the princess to get to know the unicorn? How many days before she came to love him?

In the tide of hours they bathed in dew, ran with butterflies, galloped, her arms locked around his neck. Or just spoke silently of love, she sitting in the grass, he lying at her feet.

But the three moons were running out. The night before the appointed day the king went to his daughter's room to remind her of her promise. He glanced in the corners suspiciously, sniffed the air. But the unicorn, who only ate lilies, smelled like a flower, and, hidden among the princess's gowns, blended in with the velvets, blended in with the scents.

Tomorrow is the day. I expect you to keep your word, said the king. I shall come for the unicorn at sunset.

After the king left, the princess's tears rolled down the unicorn's hide. She must obey her father, she must keep her word. Her love she must save.

Not knowing what to do, the princess picked up her lute and sang her sorrow all night long. The moon grew dim. Once again the sun filled the blossoms with light. And, as on the first day they met, the princess drew close to the unicorn. And, as on the second day, she searched the depths of his eyes. And, as on the third day, she held his head in her hands. And on the final day she drew his head to her breast, pushing with gentle strength, with the strength of love, driving the ivory thorn into her heart, blooming at last.

When the king came to claim what had been promised, this is what the dying sun delivered to him, the rose of blood and a spray of lilies.

A True Blue Idea

One day the king had an idea.

It was the first in his entire life, and he was so taken with this true blue idea that he didn't even consider telling the ministers about it. He went down to the gardens with it, ran through the grass with it, played hide-and-seek among his other thoughts with it, always returning to it with the same joy, his beautiful true blue idea.

They played together until the king fell asleep against a tree.

He woke groping for his crown and searching for the idea, and only then did he realize the danger. Alone while he slept, the idea, so fair and unfettered, might draw someone's attention. All this someone had to do was grab it and make off with it. It's so easy to steal an idea. Who would ever know it already belonged to somebody else?

Concealing the idea beneath his cloak, the king returned to the castle. He waited until night. When all eyes were closed, he left his chambers, crossed ballrooms, descended stairs and climbed steps, until he reached the Gallery of the Halls of Time.

Closed doors. And silence.

Which room should he choose?

The king stopped in front of each door, pondered a moment, then went on. Until he came to the Hall of Sleep.

He opened the door. In the padded room the king's feet sank up to his ankles, his gaze became entangled in gauzes, curtains, and veils that hung like webs. A dimly lit room, always the same. The king laid the sleeping idea on the ivory bed, lowered the curtains, locked the door, and left.

The key, he put on a thick chain around his neck. And never touched it again.

The years ran their course. The king had no more ideas, nor did he miss them, so busy was he reigning. He had grown old without realizing it before the polite royal mirrors, which lied to the truth. He only felt sadder and lonelier, but he never had any desire to play in the gardens again.

Only the ministers saw the king aging. When his head grew all white, they told him he could rest now, and relieved him of his mantle.

After placing the crown on the cushion, the king immediately raised his hand to the chain.

"Nobody cares what I do anymore," he said, crossing ballrooms and descending stairs on his way to the Halls of Time. "Nobody is watching me anymore. Now I can go find my beautiful idea and keep it for myself alone."

He opened the door, lifted the curtains.

On the ivory bed the idea slept, as true blue as that first day.

And, as on that first day, young, so young, a baby idea. And lovely. But the king was no longer the same king as that day. Between him and the idea lay all the time that had passed in the world out there, all the time that stood still in the Hall of Sleep. His eyes didn't see the same charm in the idea. He neither wanted to play nor laugh. What should he do with it? They could never be together as they had been that day.

Sitting on the edge of the bed the king cried his last two tears, the ones he had saved for the greatest sadness.

Then he lowered the curtains and, letting the idea sleep, closed the door forever.

Among the Leaves So Green O

The first doe he shot at,
He missed.
And the second doe he hit.
And kissed.
And the third ran away in
A young man's heart.
She's among the leaves
So green O.

Medieval folk song

The prince woke up happy. It was hunting day. The hounds bayed in the castle courtyard. He donned his leather vest and put on his boots. Beneath his window, the horses pawed the ground with their hooves. He took his gloves and went downstairs.

In the courtyard below it looked like a holiday. The harnesses and the animals' hides gleamed in the sun. And gleam did the teeth bared in laughter, the weapons, and the horns signaling the departure.

The horns and the clamor were heard in the forest too. Everyone knew they were coming. And each hid as best as they could.

Only the girl did not hide. She woke to the sound of the horns and she was bent down over the stream when the huntsmen arrived.

That was how the prince saw her. Half woman, half doe, drinking from the stream. The woman so beautiful. The doe so lithe. The woman he wanted to love, the doe he wanted to kill. If he approached would she run away? He snapped a twig, she raised her head, listening. Then the prince put an arrow in his bow, drew back the string, and shot at her right leg. And when the doe-woman's knees gave as she tried to pull out the arrow, he ran and seized her, calling out to men and hounds.

They took the doe to the castle. The doctor came, they tended to the wound. They placed the doe in a locked room.

Every day the prince visited her. Only he had the key. And each time he fell more in love. But the doe-woman only spoke the language of the forest, and the prince only knew the language of the palace.

So they spent hours gazing at each other in silence, with so many things to say.

He wanted to tell her that he loved her so much, that he wanted to marry her and keep her in the castle forever, that he would lavish clothes and jewels upon her, that he would send for the greatest wizard in the kingdom to turn her into a real woman.

She wanted to tell him that she loved him so much, that she wanted to marry him and take him to the forest, that she would teach him to like birds and flowers and that she would ask the Queen of Does to give him four lithe legs and a beautiful chestnut coat.

But the prince had the key to the door. And she did not possess the secret of words.

Every day they met. Now they were holding hands. And the day the first tear rolled down her cheek, the prince thought he understood and sent for the wizard.

When the doe woke, she was no longer a doe. Two legs only, long ones, and a white body. She tried to stand, but couldn't. The prince gave her his hand. The seamstresses came and heaped clothes upon her. The jewelers came and heaped jewels upon her. The dance masters came to teach her how to walk. All she lacked was the gift of speech. And the desire to be a woman.

It took her seven days to learn seven steps. And on the morning of the eighth day, when she awoke and saw the door open, she put together those seven steps and seven more, slipped along the hall, went down the stairs, crossed the courtyard, and ran into the forest to find her Queen.

The sun was still shining when the doe came out of the forest, doe only, no longer woman. And she began to graze beneath the windows of the palace.

Thread by Thread

Every afternoon, in the highest tower of the glass castle, Nemesia and Gloxinia worked at their embroidery.

Long was the white silk cloak the two fairies covered with blossoms, and which only one of them would ever wear.

But Gloxinia, never satisfied with her work, undid what she had done at the end of each day and began anew the next.

Nemesia, sure of hand, gave form to the foliage and flowers of a garden in which all the petals were sisters, and each day she ended her last stitch farther along.

Gloxinia's fingers were raw with so much undoing. The cloth became soiled. Beneath Nemesia's calm fingers the white cloak blossomed with flowers.

With so much doing and undoing, the thread was running out in Gloxinia's basket. And picking up the final skein, the fairy realized she had not advanced even by a tiny twig. Her sister would finish first and claim the cloak, while she would have nothing to show for her efforts.

There was no point in seeking perfection now. Forsaking her attempts at petals, Gloxinia used the last thread to embroider the silk, letter by letter, with the magic word. Nemesia barely had the time to complete her stitch and set free one more rose. Then she turned into a spider.

Now Gloxinia would have all the thread she needed.

Patiently, Nemesia spun the first strand. In Gloxinia's needle the thread worked perfectly, making her so sure-handed in her embroidery she had no need to resort to scissors. For the first time Gloxinia went on without undoing her work.

She became enamored with her needlework. She no longer slept. She would pick a strand from the closest web and immediately plunge the needle into the cloth, singing in cadence to the obedient stitches. Thread by thread, she forgot about her sister. There was plenty of floss, the embroidery was growing ever richer, and Gloxinia worked away happily as the years passed.

Finally, the day for the last stitch came. Gloxinia completed a petal, put the finishing touches on a thorn, and realized with a smile that there was nothing left to embroider: spring had bloomed in the cloak and the silk had disappeared beneath the foliage.

Gloxinia put away the needle and rose to her feet. She would wear the cloak, at long last she would dazzle the court. She tied the long ribbons around her neck, arranged the train, and turned to the door.

But where was the door?

All around Gloxinia, Nemesia's webs. Web upon web, Gloxinia tore at them without getting anywhere, only more and more webs.

All over the court, over the halls, over the castle and the gardens, patient Nemesia went on spinning and weaving, oblivious to her sister, forever a prisoner of her silver cocoon.

The One and Only

She was beautiful, she was the daughter, she was the one and only. A king's daughter. But what good was being a princess if she had no one to play with?

Alone in the palace, she cried and cried. She didn't want dolls, she didn't want toys. All she wanted was a friend.

At night the king heard his daughter's sobs. What good is a crown if your daughter cries at night? He wanted to put an end to her sorrow. So he called the glazier and he called the frame maker. And secretly he had them make the largest mirror in the kingdom. And quietly he had them place it at the foot of his daughter's bed while she slept.

When the princess awoke, she was no longer alone. A beautiful girl, one and only, looked back at her in surprise, her hair still tousled from sleep. Quickly they both jumped out of bed. Quickly they approached each other. One smiled and said hello. The other said hello, smiling.

"Funny," one thought, "the other is left-handed."

And they both laughed.

They laughed a lot after that. Happy together, happy the same. One's play was the other's game. One's leap was the other's bounce. And when one was tired, the other slept.

The king, delighted with such cheer, ordered new toys to be made and gave them to his daughter in a basket. Animals, dolls, little houses, and a golden ball. The ball at the bottom of the basket. But so shiny it was the first toy they chose.

They rolled on the carpet with it, they flung it on the bed, they tossed it in the air. But when the princess decided to throw it for her friend to catch, the ball shattered game and friendship.

An empty frame, shards of mirror on the floor.

Sadness weighed in the eyes of the king's only daughter. She hung her head and began to cry. A tear welled up, was about to roll down, when the princess saw the face she loved so much. Not just

the face of one friend, but many faces of many friends. Not in the tear now rolling down, but in all the shards that covered the floor.

"Funny, they're all left-handed," she thought.

And they laughed.

They laughed a good bit after that. Playing with so many friends was different. Now she could choose. One day she chose one, and then tired of her. The next day she preferred another, but quickly forgot about her. Then another and another yet, until she realized there were still too few. Then she took one, threw her against the wall, and made two. She grew tired of both, stepped on them with her shoe, and made four. No longer amused by the four, she smashed them with a hammer and made eight. Annoyed with the eight, she shattered them with a rock and made twelve.

But two were smaller than one, four smaller than two, eight smaller than four, twelve smaller than eight.

Smaller, each time smaller.

So small they no longer fit her, pieces of friends with whom she could no longer play. An eye, a smile, the side of a nose. Then not even that, just the glittery dust of friends scattered all over the floor.

Alone again, the king's daughter.

Was she crying? I don't know.

She didn't want the dolls, she didn't want the toys.

She left the palace and ran through the garden to wear out her sadness. She ran and ran, but the sadness was still with her. She ran through the forest, she ran through the meadow. Then she stopped at the edge of the lake.

In the water's reflection, her friend awaited her.

But the princess no longer wanted only one friend, she wanted many, she wanted them all, those she had had and new ones she would find. She blew on the water. The friend quavered but remained one. She threw a rock at her. The friend opened up in circles but remained one.

Then the king's beautiful daughter threw herself into the water with her arms wide open, shattering the mirror into many shards, many friends that began to sink with her, disappearing beneath the ripples as the lake rearranged its surface.

Seven Years and Seven More

Once upon a time there was a king who had a daughter. He didn't have two, he had one, and since he only had this one, he loved her more than anything else.

The princess also loved her father very much, more than anything else, until the day the prince arrived. Then she loved the prince more than anything else.

The father, who didn't have anyone else to love, immediately decided the prince was no good. He had the matter investigated and found that the boy hadn't finished his studies, had no position, and his kingdom was poor. He was a nice kid, everyone agreed, but when all was said and done, he simply was not the ideal husband for a daughter whose father loved her more than anything else.

So the king sent for the princess's fairy godmother. They thought and thought, and finally came to the conclusion that the best thing to do was to put the girl to sleep. Who knows, in her sleep she might dream of someone else and forget about the prince.

No sooner said than done, they gave the girl a magic potion and she fell asleep on the spot without even saying goodnight.

They laid the girl down on a huge bed in a huge room inside another huge room at the end of a huge hall. Seven huge doors concealed the small entrance to the huge hall. They dug seven moats around the castle. They planted seven creeping vines in the seven corners of the castle. And there they put seven guards.

The prince, when he found out that his sweetheart lay sleeping under a magic spell and that they thought this would keep her from him, did not hesitate. He had a castle built with seven moats and seven vines. He lay down on a huge bed in a huge room at the end of a huge hall concealed by seven huge doors, and went to sleep.

Seven years passed, and seven more. The vines grew over everything. The guards disappeared beneath the vines. Spiders wove silver curtains over the beds in the huge rooms in the huge halls. And the prince and princess slept on in their cocoons.

But the princess dreamed of no one but the prince. In the morning she dreamed that she saw him under her window playing the lute. In the afternoon she dreamed that they sat on the veranda and he played with the falcon and the dogs while she sat at the hoop embroidering. And at night she dreamed that the moon was high in the sky and the spiders were weaving over her sleep.

And the prince dreamed of no one but the princess. In the morning he dreamed that he saw her hair through the window, and he played the lute for her. In the afternoon he dreamed that they sat on the veranda and she embroidered while he played with the dogs and the falcon. And at night he dreamed that the moon was high in the sky and the spiders were weaving their webs.

Until the day when they both dreamed the time to marry had come, and they dreamed of a wedding filled with celebration and music and dancing. And they dreamed that they had lots of children and lived happily ever after.

News and Honey

One day the king went deaf. Not as a doorpost, more like a double casement window. He could hear everything on the left side, on the right he heard nothing.

The situation was awkward. He only paid attention to the ministers who sat on one side of the throne. And in the morning, if the rooster crowed on the wrong side, His Majesty did not wake up at all and spent the entire day sleeping.

That was when he sent for the gnome of the forest, and the gnome, obedient, showed up at the court. He came flying with his little wings, and he was so tiny that even though everyone had been informed of his arrival, they nearly mistook him for some kind of insect.

He immediately hit it off with the king, and the two struck a deal. He would live in the king's right ear and repeat to him, loud and clear, everything he heard outside. In return, since he had wings, he could, if he so desired, take advantage of his kinship to bees to make a little wax and some honey in the royal ear.

The deal worked like a charm. Whatever the gnome heard he repeated loud and clear into the caverns of the ear, and together the gnome's voice and its echo reached the king, who could now hear as well as he used to, on both sides.

Time passed. King and gnome, so close to one another, became more and more intimate. By now each knew everything about the other, and it was with pleasure that the gnome shouted, and it was with pleasure that the king heard the soft buzzing of the wings making wax and honey. A certain sweetness began to spread from the royal ear to the royal head, and little by little the king became more kind-hearted. A certain benevolence began to spread from the royal cavern to the gnome, and little by little he became more kind-hearted.

That was how the first lie came about.

The prime minister gave bad news in the left ear, and the gnome, not wishing to sadden the king, passed on good news in the right ear.

That was the first time the king heard two pieces of news at the same time.

That was the first time the king chose the better news.

More followed after that.

Every time something bad was reported to the king, the gnome turned it into something good. And every time the king heard two pieces of news, he chose the better one.

Gradually the king stopped paying attention to what he heard on the left side. Even in the morning, if the rooster crowed on that side and the gnome did not repeat the rooster's call, His Majesty forgot to hear and continued to sleep peacefully until his friend awakened him.

On one side the honey flowed. On the other came worries and sorrow, and all the bad winds seemed to blow to the left of his head.

But the king had tasted the honey, and sweetness was now more important than any news. He turned crown and throne over to the prime minister. Then he called the gnome close to his mouth and softly whispered his orders to him.

Obedient as ever, the gnome flew around to the left side and, taking advantage of his kinship to bees, made a little honey and plenty of wax, with which he stopped up the king's ear forever.

Afterword

With over sixty books and numerous prizes to her name, Marina Colasanti is among Brazil's most distinguished writers. Born in Eritrea in 1937, she has lived in Libya, Italy, and Brazil, where she has resided since 1948. As a visual artist educated at the Escola Nacional de Belas Artes, she began her career working in sculpture, painting, metal engraving, and print making, but she soon turned to journalism and literature. Her artistic project spans the plastic arts, multiple literary genres, and translation, as well as stints in TV editing, newscasting, and advertising.

Colasanti first broke into print in 1968. Her diverse production includes poetry, short stories, journalistic prose sketches and columns, children's and young adult literature, and essays on literature, women, art, social problems, and love. She is frequently the illustrator of her own works as well as an accomplished translator of world literature, from Eugenides to Barthes, from Collodi, Tomasi di Lampedusa, and Moravia to Kawabata. Her work has been recognized with numerous awards, including the prestigious Jabuti Prize (seven times), the Premio Iberoamericano SM (2017), and two mentions in the IBBY (International Board on Books for Young People) Honour List, one for her translation of *Pinocchio*. Although her work has been translated into several languages, including French, German, Italian, and Spanish, and in spite of her literary stature, only a handful of her stories have appeared in English so far.

Mapping out Colasanti's trajectory entails teasing out multiple and interwoven threads. Her rich, complex body of work blends her multiple identities as painter, writer, journalist, and feminist in a unitary project whose leitmotiv is her active commitment to contemporary women's issues. Her work in this area includes serving a four-year term in Brazil's National Woman's Rights Council (1984–89). As a journalist, she contributed for years to several major Brazilian newspapers and periodicals and was an editor at *Nova*, a women's magazine comparable to *Cosmopolitan*, frequently writing about women's issues and focusing on the personal essay and the *crônica*, a distinctive Brazilian genre that could be loosely described as journalistic prose sketch. During her tenure at *Nova*, she also maintained a column devoted to readers' correspondence. Her commitment and ability to reach out to women of all ages and socioeconomic conditions, her wide audience, and her huge popularity can be traced back to these beginnings. The collections *Nada na manga* (Nothing Up My Sleeve, 1973), *A nova mulher* (The New Woman, 1980), *Mulher daqui prá frente* (A Woman from Here On, 1981), *Aqui entre nós* (Among Us,1988) and *Intimidade pública* (Public Intimacy, 1991) are representative of this facet of Colasanti's work.

Her mini short stories, or *microcontos*, a genre she is credited with developing, are a logical offshoot of her brand of literary journalism, particularly her interest in the *crônica* and her attention to language and form. Intriguing examples of what Darlene Sadlier aptly refers to as "witty provocative sketches in the fantastic tradition" are collected in *Zooilógico* (Zooillogical, 1975), *A morada do ser* (The Dwelling Place of the Self, 1978), *Contos de amor rasgado* (Torn-up Love Stories, 1986), *O leopardo è um animal delicado*

(The Leopard Is a Delicate Animal, 1998), and *Hora de alimentar serpentes* (Time to Feed the Snakes, 2013).[1]

With her first poetry collection, *Rota de colisão* (Collision Route, 1993) Colasanti began to explore the intersection of the personal and the public from a new angle while remaining faithful to her minimalist approach and continuing to refine and expand her search for maximum expressive intensity within brief compositions. The fantastic component found in Colasanti's microfiction can be viewed as a bridge to her fairy tales, which in turn reconnect with other leitmotivs in her work, such as the linguistic and formal search, a penchant for the miniature, and exploration of the relationship between cultural and gender issues. These recurring features, together with Colasanti's keen sense of irony, interest in the unconscious, and finely honed poetic language, come together to create a unique blend of the poetic and the socially conscious.

A True Blue Idea (*Uma idéia toda azul*, 1978) is Colasanti's first collection of fairy tales. Since the association between fairy tales, fantasy, myth, and discourses of subversion is well known, it is worth remembering that the book was originally published around the time when Brazil was beginning to emerge from an extended period of repression with *abertura*, the "opening" to democratization initiated by the government of General Figuereido in 1979 that would eventually lead to the fall of the military regime. Colasanti's frequent revisitations of this genre over the years and throughout political phases, however, are a testament to the prominence of fairy tales and the enduring impact of their subtly subversive charge in her cultural project.

A True Blue Idea consists of ten short and often dark fairy tales strikingly illustrated by the author with a technique known as *nankim lavado, or* ink gouache resist, which lends the final product

1 Darlene Sadlier, ed. and trans., *One Hundred Years After Tomorrow: Brazilian Women's Fiction in the 20th Century* (Bloomington: Indiana University Press, 1992), 194.

the stark look of a woodcut. All texts revisit traditional fairy-tale characters and themes to challenge received ideas, question the relationship between the individual and society, and re-create an alternate past and reality. Now in its twenty-third edition, Colasanti's first, iconic book of fairy tales, is paradigmatic of her subsequent ventures into this territory: a very personal style that draws on her predilection for an elliptical and poetic language as well as on her sensibilities as a visual artist, and a unique blending of her concern for social, ethical, and political issues with the tradition of the fantastic.

Colasanti's fairy tales enjoy a broad and diverse reading public that includes children and adults alike. In fact, while traditional critics have often placed Colasanti's tales in the category of children's literature, the author has repeatedly and emphatically rejected the present-day ghettoization of the genre:

> When I say fairy tales, I am not referring to children's stories or even to stories about fairies. I am talking about a specific literary genre characterized by its mythic content, a genre that can be placed in the category of fantastic literature. It is, of course, needless for me to remind you of the importance that fairy tales played for Freud, Jung, and Bettelheim. Very well, I write fairy tales. I also write children's books. These are two different things. Although nowadays children are the main consumers of fairy tales, in older times these stories were not written for them, nor should they be today. True fairy tales—their content rich in meanings and multiple levels of interpretation—are meant for every age. And any person.[2]

---

2 Marina Colasanti, public lecture at the University of Illinois at Urbana-Champaign, March 26, 1996, quoted in Peggy Sharpe, "A Tropical Utopia? The Brazilian Fairy Tales of Marina Colasanti," in *Daughters of Restlessness: Women's Literature at the End of the Mil-*

Along with the reformulation of the genre's audience and its implications comes the intent to plumb the uncharted depths of the unconscious. The process of creating these tales is also linked to the unconscious, and involves reaching an "empty space," a process Colasanti has described as sailing along the single third bank of a river, or an "internal *tokonoma,*" referring to the built-in alcove in Japanese houses reserved for displaying objects for artistic appreciation. Yet this is no trance, and there is no magic word for reaching this place, "no abracadabra"; rather, it is a heightened receptive state of creativity akin to synesthesia in which "one stimulus works as a trigger for another," allowing sentences, actions, and images to expand into a new narrative.[3]

Colasanti's protagonists are classic fairy-tale fixtures such as princesses, kings, and unicorns, but only include two fairies, who could more accurately be described as witches; hence the author's preference in recent years for the term "wonder tales" over fairy tales. While they harken back to the classic repertoire collected by the Brothers Grimm or Italo Calvino and are firmly rooted in the territory of imagination, outside real time and space, the quests of their characters tend to bring into question the relationship between individual and society; they are not quests of the heroic kind, but are linked to the microlevel of daily life. Indeed, fairy tales, as Colasanti reminds us, "maintain their vitality intact through the ages because they speak of the soul and of human behavior," and that is why they are ultimately about a deeper reality in spite of their fantastic grounding.[4]

---

lennium, ed. Sabine Coelsch-Foisner, Hanna Wallinger, and Gerhild Reisner (Heidelberg: Winter, 1998), 74. The present essay is deeply indebted to Sharpe's groundbreaking, insightful work on Marina Colasanti's visual and literary production.

3 Marina Colasanti, "Posfácio," in *Mais de 100 histórias maravilhosas* (São Paulo: Global, 2015), 421, 422.

4 Marina Colasanti, quoted in Fernanda Faustino, "Marina Colasanti explica por que os contos de fada marcam gerações," August 7, 2012,

Colasanti has repeatedly stated that she views her diverse production as a unified whole. Indeed, both the fluid interplay of cross-references and reverberations and the blurring of the lines separating art forms, genres, and personal experience from artistic production found in her work not only confirm this idea but, as Peggy Sharpe perceptively points out, can ultimately be traced back to the author's "transnational identity" and thus represent "the natural evolution of her experience lived at the margins of different cultures."[5]

Colasanti describes her search for a structure that contributes to creating the overarching pattern of her work using the image of mosaic fragments forming a larger panel. The predominant elements of this supporting structure are, as we have seen, thematic, stylistic, and formal, but also quite literally visual and even architectonic. An example of this visual approximation to writing is the real estate blueprint Colasanti drew to map out *A morada do ser*:

> I drew on a clipboard a blueprint, just like the ones I had become familiar with at the real estate agency [where Colasanti worked for a time]. A real estate blueprint, for those who do not know, is the sketch of a rectangle divided in as many floors as the building in question has, each divided in as many squares as the apartments you intend to sell. . . . For my book/building I established nine floors and three penthouses. On each floor, seven apartments. And in between each floor, a common area, lobby, elevator, rec room, etc.[6]

---

http://www.globaleditora.com.br/blog/ultimas/o-mundo-magico-dos-contos-de-fadas/.

5 Peggy Sharpe, "Imagens e poder: Construindo a obra de Marina Colasanti," in *Entre resistir e identificar-se: Para uma teoria da prática da narrative brasileira de autoria feminina*, ed. Peggy Sharpe (Florianópolis: Editora Mulheres; Goiânia: Editora da UFG, 1997), 47.

6 Colasanti, "Posfácio," 416.

Indeed, writing for Colasanti is directly linked to her background as a plastic artist, and involves visually assessing and selecting the elements of the composition much in the same way a painter does, something she refers to as "the writing gaze" (*o olhar que escreve*). Writing is not made of words alone; in fact, for her a story always begins with an internal sketch: "I draw it from behind my eyes before choosing the words that, like ink, will outline it on paper. First I sketch it out as a draftswoman, and then I trace it as a writer."[7]

Colasanti's work is criss-crossed with threads connecting words and images, the literary and the visual; thus it is not surprising that she often illustrates her own books. She believes that our gaze is individual and selective, and that in appraising the elements of a composition a visual artist focuses in particular on light and shadow. Peggy Sharpe notes that in her painting Colasanti "valorizes parts or details of a whole" and uses the close-up to capture the multiplicity and complexity of life and human beings, aptly identifying metonymy as the central characteristic in both approaches.[8] This use of elliptical references containing symbolic meaning is a recurring key element in Colasanti's work and sensibility, and lies at the heart of her search for an expanded reality within a compressed space. Colasanti the visual artist and Colasanti the writer, approach their subject and their task in the same way, by seeking to achieve a synthesis through verbal economy and the metonymical displacement of images, which is akin to the close-up, and the use of light and shadow: "In my writing, I rid my text of unnecessary words and focus on scenes that I visualize in my head. In my painting, I proceed in the same way. It is as if I wanted a close-up of life, to synthesize it in its detail."[9]

---

7 Colasanti, "Posfácio," 426.

8 Peggy Sharpe, "The Blurring of Boundaries in the Life and Work of Marina Colasanti," *Women and Language* 11, no. 2 (1988): 59.

9 Quoted in Sharpe, "The Blurring of Boundaries," 59.

Colasanti's deceptively simple diction is precise, delicate, sonorous, and highly symbolic. In fact, her tales could be described as prose poetry for their heightened attention to language. The challenges of translating this genre, hybrid like the doe-woman in "Among the Leaves So Green O," are in many ways akin to those of re-creating some of the typical features of poetry: fragmentation, compression, repetition, assonance, and inverted sentence structure, among others.

A more specific problem arose with the translation of the collection's title, *Uma idéia toda azul*—literally an all blue, or bright blue, idea. Additionally, in modern spoken Portuguese *tudo azul* is a common expression that means everything is okay, peachy, cool. Puns are notoriously hard to translate, and one added complication in this case is that the connotations of this color are different in the two languages: blue is frequently associated with sadness in English, whereas the Portuguese title conveys an overall positive image of beauty and goodness. My solution was to eschew a literal translation to focus instead on the primary message—an excellent, beautiful idea—while attempting to maintain a degree of wordplay by resorting to another idiomatic expression in English that carries the implication of loyalty and, by extension, authenticity.

Other translation issues in this text are linked to basic structural differences between English and Portuguese, such as the indication of grammatical gender. While English distinguishes between masculine, feminine, and neuter personal pronouns, Portuguese lacks the latter, thus allowing for a degree of ambiguity. Such is the case with the idea of the titular tale, the unicorn, and the doe-woman, figures that straddle a fine line between animal/object and person, moving fluidly in and out of identities according to the other characters' and the reader's changing perception as the story progresses and these entities take on more human traits. Translation into English, however, requires that their role be fixed through an unambiguous choice of subject pronoun, much in the same way the girl who embroiders her sister's outline in "Through the Hoop" freezes her forever in the universe of the tapestry. I adjusted my strategy in each case, using the neuter for the idea and depending on other descriptors to convey its personification and even erotization throughout the story. For the unicorn, I opted to shift from an initial "it," dictated by the king's and princess's first, distant perception of the animal, to a successive "he" when the bond between the unicorn and the princess grows stronger. Perhaps the easiest decision was that pertaining to the doe-woman—since she is referred to as a "girl" from the beginning, the feminine pronoun seemed the most logical choice.

At times translation can also lead one down unexpected rabbit holes. Understanding the title and identifying the epigraph of "Among the Leaves So Green O" certainly falls into that category. As it turns out, both come from "The Keeper," a widely known medieval English folk song of which several more or less sanitized versions are still sung today. The deer hunt is a common symbolic image of the sexual act, and the way the song underscores this implication is also touched on in Carl Jung's *Man and His Symbols*, a work with which Colasanti was likely familiar in its Portuguese translation. Having brought the green O full circle, a final issue included reconciling the song lyrics in their multiple semantic and orthographic variations with Colasanti's own divergences in a way mindful of the integrity and individuality of a text that, like the body of its doe-woman protagonist, is joined with, but ultimately separated from, another.

I would like to thank Marina Colasanti for her friendship and for the joy and excitement reading, translating, and thinking about her art and writing continue to bring me. Thanks are also due to all the people who read and loved Marina's Little Blue Book and provided encouragement and support over the fifteen years it has taken to find a home for it, including the editorial and production team at Wayne State University Press that saw this book through to publication. Special thanks go to Fanta Ghirò, Omino Piccino Picciò, and Re Pistacchio for continued advice and inspiration. I am forever grateful to Linda and Dorian Frizzi, who introduced me to the rich world of fairy tales and to whom this translation is dedicated. This work would not have been possible without the help and support of REYoung and the Savages—thank you for continuing to share words, stories, languages, literature, and ideas, and for offering invaluable editorial and writerly input every step of the way.

Adria Frizzi

Works by Marina Colasanti in English

"Afternoon in an Empty House." Translated by Cristina Ferreira Pinto-Bailey. *Witness* 21 (2007).

"At 6 in the Evening" and "Green, however." Translated by Cristina Ferreira Pinto-Bailey. *Review. Literature and Arts of the Americas* 83 (2011).

"Family Dinner" and "Amidst Silence." Translated by Cristina Ferreira Pinto-Bailey. *Subtropics* 5 (2008).

"Life Next Door" and "A Shooting Star in the City's Sky." Translated by Rebecca Cunningham. In *Urban Voices: Contemporary Short Stories from Brazil,* edited by Cristina Ferreira Pinto. Lanham, MD: University Press of America: 1999.

"Little Girl in Red, on Her Way to the Moon." In *One Hundred Years After Tomorrow: Brazilian Women's Fiction in the 20th Century,* edited and translated by Darlene Sadlier. Bloomington: Indiana University Press, 1992.

"Through the Hoop," "The One and Only," and "The Girl Weaver." Translated by Adria Frizzi. *Delos* 32 (2017).

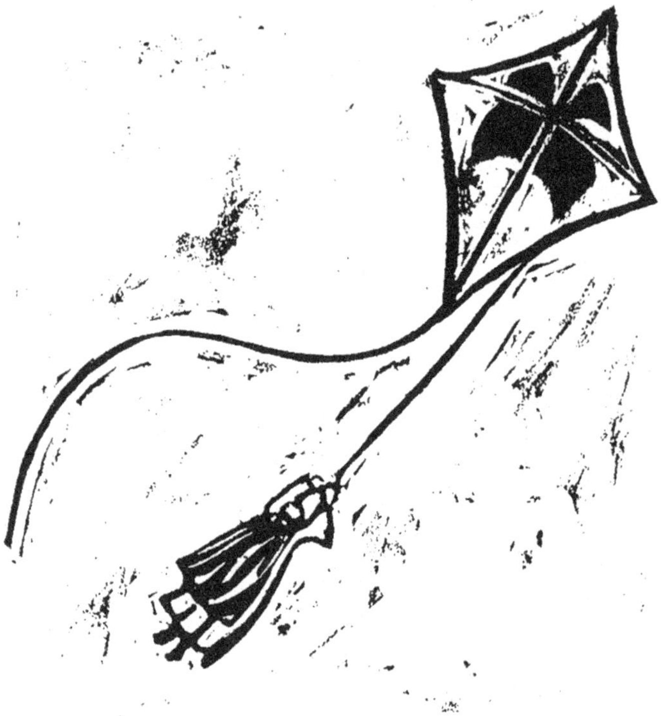

CPSIA information can be obtained
at www.ICGtesting.com
Printed in the USA
BVHW062340150119
537910BV00010B/207/P

9 780814 346396